Reader Books Weekly Reader Books Weekly

RICH MITCH

Weekly Reader Books presents

Marjorie Weinman Sharmat

RICH MITCH

illustrated by
Loretta Lustig

WILLIAM MORROW AND COMPANY
New York • 1983

This book is a presentation of Weekly Reader Books.

Weekly Reader Books offers
book clubs for children from
preschool through junior high school.
For further information write to:
Weekly Reader Books
1250 Fairwood Ave.
Columbus, Ohio 43216

1 2 3 4 5 6 7 8 9 10

Library of Congress Cataloging in Publication Data
Sharmat, Marjorie Weinman.   Rich Mitch.
Summary: Eleven-year-old Mitch finds his life turns upside down after he wins
$250,000 in the Dazzle-Rama Sweepstakes. [1. Contests—Fiction] I. Lustig,
Loretta, ill.   II. Title. PZ7.S5299Ri 1983 [Fic] 83-5398
ISBN: 0-688-02407-6

For David,
*with a million thanks
for giving me a $250,000 idea*

RICH MITCH

· 1 ·

You can't tell by looking at me that I won $250,000. Strangers don't point to me and say, "There goes the rich kid." But I'm getting pointed at just the same. Kids in school are pointing and whispering, "Did you hear about Mitch?" I'm also getting letters from people who don't know me but want to. My telephone rings all the time. Somebody named their new baby after me. Five people named their parrots after my parrot. The world has discovered Mitchell Dartmouth.

Not too long ago I had a normal life. Two parents, an older sister to fight with, a best friend, a girl in school I'd like to know better, a parrot named Dumb Dennis, and a hobby.

Maybe I should have mentioned my hobby first: I enter sweepstakes contests by mail. My sister Lynda said I reminded her of a scientist about to go mad. My mother said I should have a hobby where I could get some fresh

air. My father kept a running total of the price of my stamps on his pocket calculator. Nobody liked my hobby.

They didn't understand. I love to enter sweepstakes. I love the look of the entry blanks. I love to read "YOU MAY ALREADY HAVE WON. . . ." I love the small print that explains all the rules. I love the pictures of the prizes. I love it when our family name is printed in as if we'd already won, even though Mom says a computer does that.

I must have entered about sixty or seventy sweepstakes when I got the DAZZLE-RAMA SWEEPSTAKES in the mail. Addressed to me. I must be on a sweepstakes mailing list. I wondered if they'd cross me out if they knew I was only eleven years old. This contest was sponsored by Dazzle Detergent, the detergent that cleans and irons your clothes. But I didn't have to buy any detergent to enter. All I had to do was fill out an entry blank (print clearly and don't forget your zip code). This was a snap. A lot of the sweepstakes have numbers to match up or things to scratch off. The winning entry would be drawn from a five-foot replica of a box of Dazzle Detergent. The Grand Prize was $250,000. There were a hundred and fifty prizes in all. I entered.

The day I dropped my DAZZLE-RAMA SWEEPSTAKES entry in the mailbox was just another school day. Lynda saw the envelope in my hand as I was leaving for school and said, "Is this the day you make us filthy rich ha ha."

My mother said, "Try to get the minimum daily requirement of fresh air today."

My father totaled up my stamp expenses for the week. He said I'd make us poor trying to get rich.

I walk to school every day with my best friend, Roseanne Rich, who lives across the street. She always watches while I mail my sweepstakes entries. And she always laughs and shakes her head. "Another one," she said that day. "Don't you ever give up? You've never won anything."

"Not yet."

"It won't happen, Mitch. Do you know how many thousands of people enter those contests?"

I couldn't tell Roseanne that the numerical odds of winning the $250,000 Grand Prize in the DAZZLE-RAMA SWEEPSTAKES were one in 19,265,000. I saw it in the information sheet.

"Listen," I said, "if I win this one, I'll give you half. How about that?"

"I'm already rich."

This was Roseanne's favorite joke about her last name.

"You don't want half of what I win?" I said.

"Half of nothing. I can hardly wait." Roseanne couldn't stop laughing.

At school things weren't any better. I sit beside Melissa Gertz in some of my classes. Melissa never kidded me about the sweepstakes because Melissa never spoke to me. She's one of those stuck-up girls who only talk to certain kids. I wasn't one of them. I wished

I was. We'd been sitting side by side for two months. Sometimes she'd turn her head and look at me as if I were dead and she was just waiting for my body to be removed. Couldn't she smile?

Once she almost smiled. It was when we were all giving talks on hobbies. Naturally I gave a talk on entering sweepstakes and how I was going to get rich. Mr. Devon, our teacher, likes me because I print neatly, so he said, "Very good, Mitchell." But the kids roared. Roseanne collects lizards, which I think is weird, but nobody laughed at her.

I tried to keep quiet about my hobby after that, but it was hard. The sweepstakes were always in my mind. I had this same dream over and over.

"Is this Mitchell Dartmouth?"

"Yes."

"Do you live at 112 Fuller Street?"

"Yes."

"And did you enter the DAZZLE-RAMA SWEEPSTAKES sponsored by Dazzle Detergent, the detergent that cleans and irons your clothes?"

"Yes."

"Congratulations. You have just won the $250,000 Grand Prize."

· 2 ·

"Is this Mitchell Dartmouth?"

"Yes."

"Do you live at 112 Fuller Street?"

"Yes."

"And did you enter the DAZZLE-RAMA SWEEPSTAKES sponsored by Dazzle Detergent, the detergent that cleans and irons your clothes?"

"Yes."

"Congratulations. You have just won the $250,000 Grand Prize."

This was not a dream. One day, four

months after I entered the DAZZLE-RAMA SWEEPSTAKES, the telephone rang. I answered it. And that was the conversation. Actually those might not have been the exact words. But it was close. It was also, I figured, a joke. "You can't fool me," I said. "Winners are supposed to be notified by mail." One of the kids from school must have been having some fun.

"This isn't a joke," the voice said. "You will be notified officially by mail."

"Just a minute," I said. I ran to get my mother. If the call was from a kid, he'd hang up when he heard Mom's voice.

"Take this, Mom."

My mother picked up the receiver. She looked puzzled. She said, "Hello. This is Mrs. Dartmouth." Then she listened.

She turned to me and asked, "Did you enter some contest about cleaning and ironing clothes?"

"Sure. I entered the DAZZLE-RAMA SWEEPSTAKES."

9

She spoke into the telephone. "If this isn't legitimate, I'm contacting the Better Business Bureau, the attorney general's office, and the Office of Consumer Affairs."

I whispered to my mother. "A real contest runs a clearance check on big winners to see if they've won before or to see if they're crooks and all that stuff."

My mother spoke into the phone again. "Mitchell says this is a phony call because you didn't run a clearance check on him."

Pause. "You *did*? We didn't notice. Oh, we're not *supposed* to notice. Isn't that rather sneaky?"

Another pause. "I see. Yes. I see. I understand. Really? *Really*? It's true? *True*?" My mother turned to me and screamed, "You won $250,000!"

I knew this wasn't a dream because my mother never screams in my dreams.

Back to the telephone. My mother was saying, "What? Oh, eleven last October. I see. Well, no real problem. It's really his money, isn't it?"

10

What was she talking about? A catch, I knew it.

"Hold on," she said to the receiver. She turned to me. "The rules say that any prize won by a minor will be awarded in the name of a parent or legal guardian. But of course Dad and I aren't going to keep *your* money."

Mom was back to the phone. "The publicity? Oh, yes, he's very photogenic."

Back to me. "They want the winner's publicity to center on you. Okay?"

"Huh?"

Mom turned back to the phone. "He says wonderful."

That's the way the conversation went. Mom talked to the man on the phone. Then she talked to me. Then back to the man on the phone. All this time she was taking off her clothes. She does that when she gets excited. First her jacket went. Then her watch. Then her shoes. She was starting on her stockings. I hoped the conversation wouldn't go on much longer.

I just stood there in shock. I couldn't be-

lieve that I won! I wondered what $250,000 looked like. If they paid you in pennies would they fill the whole room? Or the house? Or the neighborhood? What would $250,000 in nickels look like? Or dimes. What if they paid in stamps! I could plaster them all over the house. My father would go crazy trying to peel them off.

My mother would never send me out into the fresh air again.

Lynda would stop making fun of me. She'd start begging me for money.

Roseanne would stop laughing at my hobby.

Roseanne.

I had a little problem there.

I owed Roseanne Rich $125,000.

· 3 ·

"We'll owe a fortune in taxes," said my father.

These were the first words out of his mouth after my mother told him the news. He went straight to his desk and started to write down figures and cross them out and write more figures. He kept scratching his head. "A fortune in taxes," he repeated. Then he brightened up. "Still, there was only a total investment of $12.40 worth of stamps. So before taxes that's a clear profit of $249,987.60. And if we put a clever accountant to work on our problem . . . ."

"Problem?" I said.

"Yes. Being rich is complicated. It requires certain strategies. First, I think we should rename your parrot Dumb Dennis Dazzle."

"What?" I asked. "Would you repeat that slowly."

"You mean we should call him Dumb Dennis Dazzle?" asked Mom.

"No, just plain Dazzle in honor of Dazzle Detergent. We could coach him to say it. It would be a goodwill gesture toward the company that made us rich. You have to start thinking that way."

"Nothing doing," I said. "Change *your* name to Dazzle, not my parrot's."

Lynda hadn't said a word since she heard the news. "I want to move," she said suddenly. "I don't like this neighborhood. It has ants and weeds. Rich people don't have ants and weeds. They have butlers. And horses. I want a horse."

The telephone rang.

"They've changed their mind, I know it,"

said Mom. "It was a plot designed to make us all act crazy."

"They succeeded," said Dad as he answered the phone.

It was Newton. He was always calling me up to ask me to do something. I liked Newton but I wished he wouldn't hang around me all the time.

Dad handed me the receiver.

"Hi. Whatcha doing?" Newton asked.

"Nothing."

"Wanna do something?"

"I can't."

"Why?"

Newton always had to know why I couldn't do something.

"I'm busy."

"I thought you said you were doing nothing."

"Next week, Newton, okay?"

"Well, okay. Call me back if things loosen up."

The minute I got through with Newton, the telephone rang again.

"It's the Dazzle death knell," said Lynda. "We're as poor as we were an hour ago."

"We're not poor," said Dad.

"Ever taken a good look at this dump?" said Lynda.

"Stop it," said Mom. "Dazzle is *supposed* to call back. About arrangements for a big ceremony to give Mitchell the money. It's all coming back to me now."

I answered the phone. Roseanne was on the other end.

"I can't find my homework notes from English. Can I borrow yours?"

"Sure."

"Great. I'll be right over."

"No!"

"No?"

"Uh, I'll bring them right over. Mitchell's Delivery Service on the way. Bye."

"That was fast," Mom said.

"Mitchell's Delivery Service?" said Lynda. "Are you starting up a new business with the money you won?"

"I have to go over to Roseanne's," I said.

17

"Why didn't you tell her your big news?" asked Mom.

"I don't want to brag. Maybe she'll never find out. Why does she have to know?"

"Modesty, modesty," said Lynda.

"Well, you *can't* keep it a secret," Mom said. "Mr. Hemingway, the man who called with the news, said it's going to be on TV."

"What? You mean *everybody* is going to know about this?"

"Everybody who watches TV and reads a newspaper and listens to the radio. Don't you want everybody to know you won?"

"Well, not every single person in the world. *Most* people, but not everybody."

Mom went on. "Roseanne will be one of the first to know, even if you don't tell her, because she'll see the limousine drive up. She lives just across the street. How can she miss it?"

"A limousine?"

"Yes. Oh, isn't this exciting?"

"Hey, Mitch, you're really a big shot." This

was from Lynda. She didn't sound happy about it.

I took my homework notes over to Roseanne's. I watched her while she read them. Should I tell her and get it over with? Just like that I'd lose $125,000. She'd find out anyway. Still, I couldn't be positive. And if I waited I might be able to figure out a plan. I wasn't going to make a $125,000 decision in a minute.

"Are you happy, Roseanne?" I asked, before I could catch myself.

"Sure. I guess. Why?"

"What if you were rich or something? Would you be happier?"

"I am rich or something."

"Come on. I mean if you had lots and lots of money. Wouldn't it make any difference to you?"

"Sure. But why all these questions about money?"

"It's on my mind."

"It's always on your mind, Mitch."

Roseanne handed my notes back to me. "Are you okay? You look kind of strange."

"Sure I'm okay," I said. "See you tomorrow."

I was glad to get back to my house where everybody knew I won $250,000. But they didn't know I had promised to give half of it away. I felt angry. I was angry at Roseanne for being so nice. I was angry at Dazzle Detergent for putting me in this spot. And I was angry at myself for making a bad promise. And not keeping it.

"Mr. Hemingway called again," Mom said as I walked in the door. "He said the limousine is coming to our house after school Friday afternoon. Going from school to wealth in one afternoon has a lot of human interest, he said. We're all being driven to Dazzle headquarters in New York for the ceremony. They would have flown us to New York if we didn't live in the suburbs."

"So they owe us a plane trip. I always wanted to go to California."

"Don't interrupt," said Mom. "The media

will be there on Friday afternoon for the check-giving ceremony. Then on Saturday the limo is coming again and so is a TV crew to record your new haircut and new clothes."

"I don't need a haircut or clothes."

"It's going to be a feature on the *Have a Good Day* television show," said Mom.

"Why would anyone want to see me getting a haircut?"

"Because people are interested in an eleven-year-old boy who won $250,000."

"They're interested in his haircut?"

"That's right," said Dad.

"I like my hair the way it is and it only cost three dollars."

"Wait till you see what fifty dollars will do to it," said Mom.

"It's a fifty-dollar haircut?"

"Dazzle is paying for it."

"Does that mean it gets cleaned and ironed, too?"

"Don't kid around," said Lynda. "I'd kill for a fifty-dollar haircut."

"Take mine," I said. "I mean it."

21

"You're the winner," said Dad, "so it's your head people are interested in."

"I want Lynda to have a fifty-dollar haircut, too." I felt like a big shot. "I insist."

"Hey, you're all right, Mitch," said Lynda.

This was the second nice thing Lynda had said to me in one day. A new record. Is that what money can do? I wondered what Melissa Gertz would think of me now.

The fantastic thing that had happened was just starting to hit me. Maybe a fifty-dollar haircut was right for a winner like Mitchell Dartmouth. I no longer had a three-dollar head.

·4·

Two men from Dazzle Detergent arrived Friday afternoon right after I got home from school. Mom had fixed up our place to make them feel at home. She went out and bought boxes and boxes of Dazzle Detergent and stood them up all over the house.

It looked silly. I had never seen boxes of detergent in a fireplace. How about three on a couch? One on top of the piano? "It looks loyal," said Mom.

Dad was now carrying around a little note-book in which he was constantly marking

down figures. When he saw the boxes of detergent he whipped his notebook out of his pocket. He mumbled while he marked down figures. "Seventeen boxes of detergent at $4.39 per box adds up. It's not the best use of our funds. Then again we could try washing our clothes with the stuff afterwards." Dad closed his notebook. "I'd say it was a risky investment."

The men from Dazzle pulled up in a limousine driven by a chauffeur in a uniform. The limousine was long and black and sleek. Mom, Dad, Lynda, and I were looking out the window watching it drive up to our house. "We shouldn't be doing this," said Lynda. "We have to start acting classy. We've got about one minute to get rid of these gross detergent boxes. Rich people don't have detergent boxes in their living rooms."

"They stay," said Mom. "When you're older you'll recognize atmosphere when you see it."

"They make me sneeze," said Lynda.

I was busy looking across the street. Nobody was at the windows of Roseanne's house. So far, so good.

Mom let the two Dazzle guys into the house. There were five boxes of Dazzle just inside the front door. The men didn't seem to notice. The man in front grabbed my hand, shook it up and down, and kicked over a box of detergent. He didn't look down. He introduced himself as "the man on the telephone, Roger Hemingway. That's Hemingway as in Ernest. Everyone calls me Rog. I'm vice-president of marketing for Dazzle Detergent."

Rog was ticking off items about himself like someone describing a product. Then he introduced the man in back of him as "Al." I guess Al didn't have a title. He was a no-frills brand. Al's job was to stand behind Rog.

Rog and Al looked at all the boxes of detergent. "What a dazzling idea," said Rog.

I heard Lynda groan.

Mom gestured for Rog and Al to sit down. They each took a chair, since the sofa was occupied. They checked for spilled detergent before sitting.

26

Rog spoke to me. "Young man, we have big plans for you. This afternoon you'll be given your check at our corporate headquarters. The media will be there. Tomorrow a television crew will follow you around while you get a haircut and new clothes. You're a very lucky young man."

"I like to have my hair shorter on the sides than on the top," I said, "because hair on your ears can make them itch and . . . ."

Rog kept right on talking. "But before we get going, I'd like to get a bit of background information on you and your family."

He and Al took turns asking us about a hundred questions. Rog's last question was, "How does it feel to win $250,000, Mitchell?"

"Feels real good," I said.

I think he wanted a better answer than that.

"What do you plan to do with the money?" asked Al.

I wanted to give Al a great answer. Maybe I could earn him a title or a last name.

But Mom spoke up. "That's to be determined," she said. "By wiser heads than ours."

27

"Very prudent," said Rog.

"I'm pretty wise for my age," I said.

"I'm sure you *are,*" said Rog. "Well, shall we move on? The ceremony is scheduled for four o'clock."

"Does that mean we'll be on television tonight?" asked Lynda.

"No, the *Have a Good Day* show will broadcast it a week from tomorrow. Some of the footage will be released to the networks for their news broadcasts."

"You mean all over the country?" I asked.

"All over the free world," said Rog.

"Fabulous," said Mom.

"You're going to be famous, young man," said Rog.

"Not *too* famous, I hope," said Dad.

"But we're prepared for fame," said Mom, who looked like she was getting hot. "That is, we can handle it without going to pieces." Mom took off her ring and her watch. She was fiddling around with her belt.

"What my wife means," said Dad, "is that

28

there are so many opportunists out there who would love to, shall we say, 'share' our money."

When Dad said share the money, I cringed. What would happen when he found out about Roseanne! At least the news wouldn't break until next week. That would give me a whole week to figure out what to do about Roseanne. Our accountant had already estimated that we'd have to pay at least seventy-five thousand dollars in taxes. Subtract the taxes and Roseanne's share from my prize, and I was left with about fifty thousand. Rog didn't look like the kind of person who would make a fuss over a mere fifty thousand dollars. He'd walk out the door if he knew the truth.

Rog noticed my parrot in his cage over in a corner.

"Does your parrot talk?"

"His name is Dumb Dennis," I said. "He's never said a word. But he's a wonderful pet."

"He *looks* wonderful," said Rog. "You must be very proud of him."

29

I began to doubt that Rog was a sincere person.

"Why not bring the parrot along?" said Al. "It's a good angle."

"I agree," said Dad. "Excellent strategy."

Rog was staring at Dumb Dennis. "A family pet. Very heartwarming, very marketable. And a nice change from dogs. Dogs are so common." Rog stood up. "Well, shall we leave?"

We all started to walk toward the door.

"Don't forget the bird," said Rog.

Dad carried Dumb Dennis in his cage. He was whispering to him. "*Dazzle. Dazzle. Dazzle. Remember what I taught you. You can say it. You're smart, Dumb Dennis.*"

We locked the house and walked out to the limousine.

The chauffeur opened the door for us. Mom peered inside. "This is spectacular!"

"Nothing is too good for the $250,000 kid," said Rog.

As we got into the limousine, for one crazy moment I wanted Roseanne to be looking.

· 5 ·

I wore a new shirt washed in Dazzle for the ceremony. That was another of my mother's ideas. She wanted to be able to say truthfully, "Mitchell's shirt was washed in Dazzle." The shirt was so new it had never been worn. It looked clean *before* it went into the wash. And it sure looked more ironed than when it came out. Dazzle claims to iron your clothes, but it doesn't say what they look like afterwards.

The Dazzle corporate offices were in a New York skyscraper. After our elevator ride we got ushered from room to room and up and down stairs. All along the way we were intro-

31

duced to people. Everyone acted as if they knew me very well. But they paid more attention to Dumb Dennis. At last we were in this big room with television cameras. There were lots of people standing around. There was a uniformed man and about a dozen well-dressed men and women plus the television crew.

I was told to stand next to this tremendous box of Dazzle. I bet there wasn't any Dazzle in it. The box and I were about the same height. My parents and Lynda stood just behind me.

"Hold up the bird cage, Mr. Dartmouth," Rog said. "Higher, please."

Dad looked proud. He hoisted the cage above his head.

"A bit lower, Mr. Dartmouth," said Rog.

While Dad was raising and lowering the cage, Lynda was trying to peek into the Dazzle box. I was standing under a spotlight. There were other lights all over the place. It was hot.

Rog motioned to the television people. They started to zoom in on me. Suddenly a man appeared from behind a curtain and stuck something in my hand. His voice boomed out "Congratulations!" He shook my hand. He kept shaking it while the cameras moved in closer. Unfortunately he was shaking the hand that was holding the check. I could feel the check squashing.

Rog was signaling me with his arms. He wanted me to hold up the check for the camera. I held it up. Rog made a face. Dazzle, the detergent that washes and irons your clothes, sure awarded one wrecked check.

Rog waved for the cameras to stop. "Could we do that again, please, with a fresh check?"

"You mean I get another $250,000?" I asked.

Rog tried to smile. "The computer would have a heart attack."

Rog and the check man put their heads together. "We'll be right back," Rog announced. They returned a few minutes later. The check man was holding a piece of paper. It looked like a check from where I was standing.

Rog turned to the television people, "We're

doing the ceremony again. But don't go beyond this spot." Rog drew an imaginary line on the floor.

The check man went behind the curtain and walked out again. He stuck the paper in my hand. This time he didn't shake my hand.

Rog signaled for me to hold up the paper. He signaled the television crew not to come any closer.

I looked up at the paper I was holding. It was smooth and crisp. It said, FIVE DOLLAR DISCOUNT COUPON FOR MOE'S UP-TOWN GARAGE.

Rog signaled to Mom and Dad and Lynda. I got hugs and kisses for the camera. Dad gave me a half hug because he was holding up Dumb Dennis's cage with one hand.

Suddenly Dumb Dennis squawked, "Dazzle!"

"Beautiful!!!" said Rog. "This, ladies and gentlemen, is Dumb Dennis, the family pet."

All the cameras zoomed in on Dumb Dennis while I just stood there holding my discount coupon.

"Say something else, Dennis." A reporter stood by the cage with a tape recorder.

"Speech, speech," said another reporter.

You'd think Dumb Dennis had won the sweepstakes.

Dumb Dennis clammed up. So the reporters turned to me and asked what I planned to do with the money. I answered before my parents could say a word. "Well, I'll probably give two hundred thousand of it to my favorite charities. The fifty thousand that's left I keep for myself."

Mom looked mad, and I was afraid she was going to start taking off her clothes then and there. She was. She removed her belt and kicked off a shoe. Dad nudged her. "Not *here*," he said. "You'll get arrested." Dad was mad at me, too. He muttered, "Two hundred thousand dollars to *charity*!"

Lynda whispered to me, "You promised me the haircut."

When it was over, Rog said, "I hope you won't get pestered by a bunch of characters wanting some of your money."

"I don't have any money," I said. "I have a discount coupon from Moe's Uptown Garage. Where is my check?"

"*What*? Where did it go?"

"That's what I'm asking you. I think you dropped it on the floor."

The television cameras started to roll while Mom, Dad, Lynda, me, the check man, Rog, and most of the well-dressed men and women of Dazzle got down on their hands and knees to look for the check.

Somebody found it in the replica of the Dazzle Detergent box. We were trying to figure out how it got there when Dumb Dennis squawked, "Dazzle!" again.

The cameras zoomed in on him.

Dumb Dennis had turned into a big show-off.

·6·

The hairdresser's name was Ormanne and he had eaten garlic for lunch. It was hard to duck when he breathed on me because he was supposed to stand over me and do things to my hair. Since cameras were going at the same time and notes were being taken, he wanted to talk.

"Who cut your hair last?" he asked with disgust. "You have patches of short hair, patches of long hair, and a cowlick that has been allowed to run wild. I would take away that hairdresser's license."

"Mom cuts it between visits to the barber."

"Your mother!" said Ormanne. "I should have known. Mothers whip out their little haircut kits and congratulate themselves on the pennies they're saving by massacring their children's hair."

"Fifty bucks isn't pennies, Ormanne."

Ormanne glared at me.

I didn't like him. "Did *your* Mom grow the garlic you had for lunch?" I asked.

Some of the people around us were laughing. Some weren't. These included Mom and Rog.

I was afraid Ormanne would dye my hair purple for revenge. But he just kept snipping. We were in a private room at his styling salon. It was at a fancy address in New York City. The wallpaper was all silvery and shiny. It looked like the room was enclosed in aluminum foil, like a sandwich. I found out afterward that Dazzle didn't pay for the haircut because Ormanne and his salon were getting free nationwide publicity.

My hair kept falling and falling onto this silvery sheet that was around my shoulders. More and more hair. Suddenly I knew what his revenge plan was. He was going to make me bald! Why did I mention garlic!

There was a mirror in front of me but I didn't want to look. I could feel Ormanne's hands all over my head as he swept up clumps of hair. At last he stopped cutting and started combing. Then he grabbed a container and started to spray my hair. The stuff smelled awful. This was his revenge. I was going to smell like a bunch of lilacs for the rest of my life.

The cameras moved in closer.

"Open your eyes and look in the mirror," Ormanne commanded.

I looked. I didn't recognize myself. I was all smooth and slick. And I seemed to have more hair than when we started. A person has to be a genius to cut off all that hair and leave a kid with more hair than he started with.

"Well . . . ." said Ormanne.

"It's great," I said.

Ormanne smiled. At the cameras.

"It's called The Clip," he said to the cameras. "I originated it."

Ormanne handed me a silver-colored slip of paper with printing on it. "It comes with a list of instructions. If you follow them exactly, you should get a week's wear out of this cut."

"What happens the second week?"

Ormanne didn't answer.

The television crew filmed us as we got back in the limousine and were driven off. Rog followed us in their van.

"I can hardly wait for them to film you trying on your new clothes, Mitchell," said Mom.

"Wait a minute. Do they go into dressing rooms? Do they see you in your underwear?"

"That won't get on television," said Dad. "They only use a small part of what they film, and I'm sure they won't use *that*."

"This is getting good," said Lynda.

"Hair is one thing, but nobody gets a peek at me in my underwear."

The chauffeur, who had not spoken a word to us, suddenly turned around and said, "No underwear shots."

"Whew!"

The store was crowded. "You go first," Rog said. My family and Rog and Al and the television crew followed me like a parade. Everyone stared at us. At *me*. I liked this much better. I loved it! The cameras were focused on me alone. I was dressed like a slob because Rog said that would make my "transformation" more interesting.

The store didn't sell anything for less than a hundred dollars. Maybe some socks. We marched toward the boys' department. Rog and Al led the way.

A boy came up to me. "Can I have your autograph?" he asked. He was holding a piece of paper. Another boy was with him. "Who's he?" the second boy asked.

"I don't know," the first boy answered.

Rog put his arm on my shoulder. "This is Mitchell Dartmouth. He just won $250,000 in the DAZZLE-RAMA SWEEPSTAKES."

"Is DAZZLE-RAMA a video game?" asked the second boy.

"No," I said.

The boys shrugged and walked away.

Mom rushed up to me. "Your first autograph!" she said. "Isn't that exciting."

"They didn't want it," I said.

"But they *almost* wanted it, son," said Dad.

"They'll kick themselves when they see you on *Have a Good Day*," said Rog.

"I'll bet," said Lynda.

I was glad to get to the dressing room where I could pull the curtain.

· 7 ·

We couldn't deposit the check until Monday. We spent all day Sunday looking at it. It was wrinkled and gray. But it said $250,000. The check was made out to my parents. "Just a legal formality," Mom said. Then she started to scream. Lynda and I looked at her with horror. "Why not?" Lynda said. She screamed, too. Dad and I joined in. People should scream more often. It's really fun. The only real fun we had so far.

On Monday morning Mom took the check to the bank. Dazzle had made arrangements so the bank wouldn't arrest her.

I went to school as usual. Nobody knew I had won the sweepstakes. Roseanne asked if I was feeling okay. She asked me that every day. Melissa didn't crack a smile. Newton pestered me. Everything was just about the same. And it stayed that way until Saturday.

On Saturday we took our telephone receiver off the hook to watch *Have a Good Day*. I don't know why *Have a Good Day* is on at night. It's one of the top-rated shows in the country, Rog said. It's an hour program and we kept thinking our part would be next. Finally there were only seven minutes left. Hardly time for Ormanne's haircut. Suddenly, there we were!

You could see me holding up the discount coupon from Moe's Uptown Garage. That lasted about a split second. Then a close-up of Dumb Dennis filled the screen. That seemed to last forever. Then back to me saying, "I'll give two hundred thousand of it to my favorite charities."

My mother gasped.

Next there was a scene of Mom, Dad,

45

Dumb Dennis, Lynda, and me together.

"I look gross!" Lynda covered her eyes.

"Didn't I shave?" Dad asked himself.

"Wasn't I wearing a belt?" asked Mom.

Dumb Dennis was back on the screen. He squawked, "Dazzle!"

"Hey, they paid more attention to Dumb Dennis than me," I said.

"Don't take it personally," said Dad. "A parrot who squawks 'Dazzle' is simply more marketable. Understand, Mitchell?"

"No."

"They're building an advertising campaign around the Dazzle Parrot."

"They like him better than me?"

"No, it's just that he can say Dazzle."

"So can I."

I turned back to the program. I wondered if there would be a scene of everybody on their hands and knees hunting for the check. There wasn't. A commentator was saying, "And here's Mitchell at Ormanne's Silver Streak Styling Salon."

46

Yuck!

Ormanne hardly had time to breathe on me before the film showed me at the clothing store. The two boys who almost wanted my autograph were in it! The commentator's voice was saying, "Mitchell is asked for his very first autograph." They cut out the part where the boys walked away without it. The film ended with me standing with my mother and father and Lynda. At least it looked like the end. Suddenly there was Dumb Dennis again!

"He didn't go to those places with us," I said.

Dumb Dennis squawked, "Dazzle!" and the show was over.

"Did I look okay?" asked Lynda.

"You looked okay, honest," I said.

"I did?"

Actually I only got a quick look at Lynda. I was too busy looking at myself. Ever since I won the contest, Lynda had been pushed in the background. Maybe she wasn't exactly pushed in the background. I just got pushed up front. I hoped she didn't hate me.

My mother put the receiver on the hook.

Nobody called. For an hour. Then the telephone went wild. We got one call after another. From friends and relatives and people who claimed to be friends or relatives.

At midnight we took the receiver off again.

"We'll put it back Sunday noon," said Mom.

"Let's lock the doors tight tonight," said Lynda.

"You think someone will try to break in?" I asked.

Mom and Dad looked worried.

"Tell you what," said Dad. "I'll lock the doors and the rest of you go around and double-check them. Also the windows."

"I want to go to a hotel," said Lynda. "A hotel for rich people."

"Let's just go to sleep," I said. "I'm tired."

The next morning we all complained that we didn't sleep well the night before. "Nobody broke in," said Dad.

"I wish I knew that last night before it didn't happen," said Lynda.

The doorbell rang.

"Hide the silver," said Lynda.

"Who is it?" I called out.

"It's me. Roseanne."

Roseanne! She didn't come for the silver. She came for $125,000.

I let Roseanne in. "I'm so excited I could scream," she said.

"We already did that," said Lynda.

"When I saw you on *Have a Good Day*, I wanted to rush right over. But I didn't want to bother you last night. I'm sorry I didn't have more faith in you. Mitch, I wish you had told me the second you won. I guess you had to keep it a secret until the program went on."

"He didn't *have* to," said Lynda.

Roseanne was going on and on about the sweepstakes. She *should* be excited. She was as much a winner as I was. I kept waiting for her to say, "I've come for my half." But she didn't.

The telephone rang.

"Who put the receiver back on?" asked Mom.

"Guilty," said Lynda. "I just thought somebody might call *me*."

· 8 ·

The news was all over school on Monday. I couldn't even *get* to school without having kids mob me. They hung around kidding me. "Hey, can I borrow a million dollars? Can you spare a nickel for a new car?" Corny jokes, but I loved them. Roseanne still didn't say anything about her share of the money.

When I got to school, I couldn't believe my popularity. A couple of big-shot athletes, guys I didn't even know, stopped me in the hallway. "Hey, you're famous," one of them said. Only Newton stayed away. Funny. I thought

51

he'd be like flypaper. But he slunk away as if he was afraid I wouldn't recognize him.

In class I sat down beside Melissa as usual, wondering what she would do. I didn't have to wait long. She smiled! Not a quarter of an inch on one side or something like that. This was a real smile. I smiled back.

Some more kids came over and said, "Hey, TV star." Some of them paid more attention to my being on TV than my winning the money.

After they left, Melissa said, "Hi." I said, "Hi." Then I thought, maybe she had been shy. Maybe that's why she had been treating me like a dead person.

"Do you like avocado sandwiches?" she asked. "Celebrities like avocado sandwiches."

"How do you know that?" Melissa was still smiling at me.

"I know about famous people. The first time I ever saw you I knew you were going to be famous."

I felt like squirming. Why did I feel like squirming?

Class started. Melissa smiled at me steadily over the next hour.

After school I ran home. When I got there, I saw Lynda standing frozen outside our fence. A ferocious dog was inside the fence. "Do we own a dog?" she asked.

"A dog?"

"In particular, this vicious monster who won't let me into my own house."

Just then a frantic face appeared at our living room window. And a frantic hand waving us away from the house.

"It's Mom! She's trapped inside!" I said.

"Let's call the police," said Lynda. "Mom's scared inside and we're scared outside. And we don't even know what's going on."

The dog was a Doberman pinscher. He looked like something you'd see guarding a state prison. You could easily believe he had just eaten the warden.

The dog started to wag his tail. Maybe he was friendly! I love dogs. Next to parrots, they're my favorite pets. But Mom doesn't like dogs. She says they're trouble. She says that every time she gets near one, she feels like taking her clothes off.

This dog kept wagging his tail. I was thinking, he wants to be *my* dog. "I bet he's our new watchdog," I said. "Dad bought him."

"I prefer Dumb Dennis," said Lynda.

"We could throw this dog some food with a tranquilizer in it," I said. "That's what crooks do when they rob a house that has a guard dog."

"Forget it. I'm going across to Roseanne's house and call the police."

"No," I said. "Just call Dad. He'll know what to do."

"Okay."

Twenty minutes later, Dad arrived. He took one look at the dog, one look at Mom's frantic face and waving hand, and he knew just what to do.

He called the police.

·9·

It was kind of sad to see the police take the dog away. It would have been sadder if the dog hadn't tried to nip one of the policemen.

Sergeant Grimes stayed behind to explain about the dog.

"There was a note attached to his collar," he said. He handed it to me. We all took turns reading it.

Please accept Lambykins with my compliments. If you feed him raw liver and treat him as a member of your family, he will protect your home and loved ones from evildoers.

I left Lambykins behind your fence to show you

just how vulnerable your house is to strangers.
Newly rich people are the most vulnerable of all.

God bless you.

A Friend.

"What's going to happen to Lambykins?" I asked Sergeant Grimes.

"He has a license tag. We'll trace his owner."

"What happens if the owner doesn't want him back?"

"Well . . . ."

"You'll destroy the dog, isn't that right?"

"He'll be put up for adoption. If anyone is crazy enough . . . ." Sergeant Grimes stopped.

"Someone might want him," I said. "He's beautiful in a monstrous sort of way."

"I don't get it," he said. "Why would anyone leave this dog with you?"

"Because I'm rich and famous and need a guard dog, I guess."

I told the Sergeant about the sweepstakes.

"Oh, *you're* the one who won," he said.

"I heard about that. Best wishes."

"Can I call you to see if you've found the dog's owner?"

"Sure. Just call the station and ask for me."

Sergeant Grimes left.

I went into the house. "You have three requests for local interviews," Mom said. "But I don't think you should rush into them. It might spoil your national image."

"I agree," said Dad. "We can't say yes to everything. We have to be clever about situations and people and more importantly about money. We have to give serious thought to investing the money we won."

"*I* won," I said.

"Of course," said Dad. "Well, tomorrow when your mom and I get together with our accountant, we'll try to pin down exactly how much money will be left after taxes. We'll take a hard look at our financial picture."

Maybe this was a good time to tell them about Roseanne. She was going to be a very big part of the financial picture. But I didn't say anything.

·10·

We got sacks of mail. Most of the letters were addressed to me, but my parents also received a lot of mail. Lynda got a few letters and so did Dumb Dennis.

One night we sat around and opened up all the mail. This was my first letter:

Dear Mitchell,
Do you know what it's like to be fat? I am writing in behalf of my widowed aunt, victim of a rare metabolic disease which causes her to gain five pounds every month. Do you think she

overeats? No! She starves herself. Fatties Anonymous has done nothing to help her condition. Doctors have failed to find a cure. The Pratt Clinic in Boston, the Mayo Clinic in Minnesota and the Cleveland Clinic in Ohio have depleted her meager savings. But now there is a ray of hope! Doctors in the famed Strogonoff Institute in Moscow have found a cure. But it costs money. I am asking you, Mitchell, to open your heart to my aunt in her desperate and courageous struggle against the agony of fat. The air fare (tourist class) and other expenses to send my aunt and me (my aunt cannot eat unassisted) to Moscow will total $9,546.

A personal interview with my aunt can be arranged if you wish.*

Desperately yours,
Sanford LeBean, nephew
P.O. Box 8801
Tucson, Arizona 85715

*Round-trip air fare for two between Tucson, Arizona, and New York: $832.60, tax included.

I read the letter out loud. "What'll I do?" I asked. "Do you think she's really that fat?"

"Do you think she really exists?" said Lynda.

"I could investigate," I said. "I could hire a private detective."

"Here, read the next letter," said Lynda. "It's air mail and it's on lavender stationery."

Dear Fellow Pet Lover,
Congratulations on winning the
DAZZLE-RAMA SWEEPSTAKES! And
even heartier congratulations on
possessing such a sweet and generous
nature. Alas, you must be hearing from
numerous individuals concerning your
desire to donate $200,000 to charity. I
know how difficult it must be to separate
the truly worthwhile letters from those
written by people trying to take your

hard-earned winnings for their own selfish gain or frivolous projects. I do sympathize.

You will be pleased to know, therefore, that I am not a charity. I am, in fact, writing to you as a fellow pet owner. Yes! Isn't it marvelous to own a little furry or feathered creature! I commend you on your devotion to your parrot, Dumb Dennis. But alas! Our loved ones are not with us forever. Therefore, I am writing to ask you to join me in my new venture, a pet cemetery. Also, I am engaging a local all-boys chorus to ensure that funeral services become a meaningful ritual. A video cassette of the ceremony will provide a lasting momento. A full-colored photograph of the deceased pet in his final repose will be provided for the bereaved.

Now here is the most exciting news of all!!!! I propose to name the cemetery after your pet, the DUMB DENNIS

PET MORTUARY. A contribution of $30,000 will entitle your parrot to a marble mausoleum in Parrot Gardens.

Please make your check or money order payable to Thelma Scrinch. I shall, of course, deposit it in the DUMB DENNIS PET MORTUARY account. Viva la pets!!!!

Yours,
Thelma Scrinch
Victoria Station
New South Wales,
Australia

We were all quiet. Then Mom said, "Well, you're international, Mitchell."

"I love Dumb Dennis," I said. "But I'm more worried about a fat person than a dead parrot."

"Mitchell," said Dad, "did it ever occur to you that this beany guy or whatever his name is, just wants your money?"

"Sure. You think I'm stupid?"

"No. Just soft-hearted," said Dad.

"Read us another one, Mitch," said Lynda.

I opened the next envelope, and a photograph fell out. It was a picture of a boy. Pasted on the picture was a note: THIS CHILD IS STARVING. There was a letter in the envelope, too.

"Here goes," I said.

Dear Mitchell,

Meet little Ronnie. This unfortunate boy is eleven years old, just like you. But he's not lucky like you. Little Ronnie's father left when Ronnie was just two days old. The following day, Ronnie's father was joined by Ronnie's mother. Since then, it's been orphanages and foster homes for poor little Ronnie. But now, YOU can adopt Ronnie as your little brother for only $100 a month.

Send your contribution to
SAVE RONNIE FUND
SUITE 100-A
SYCAMORE TOWERS
BEVERLY HILLS, CALIFORNIA

P.S. An extra few dollars each month will buy a little treat for Ronnie. Food, shoes, a roof over his head, anything that more fortunate children take for granted.

Mom picked up the boy's picture and stared at it.

"That's Lance Davenport!" she shrieked. "He starred in *Hunger City* twenty-five years ago."

"How could he do that if he's only eleven?"

"Eleven?" said Mom. "He's thirty-five if he's a day."

"I guess you could say this letter is a phony," I said.

"I guess you could say that," said Dad.

"Creeps," said Lynda. "The world is full of creeps. Hey, what's this?" She held up a small envelope. "This looks like an invitation," she said. "Wanna bet the admission fee is ten thousand dollars?"

Lynda opened the envelope. "Well, well, well."

"What does *that* mean?" I asked.

"This one's legitimate. Melissa Gertz's inviting you to a party."

"Hey, give me that. It's my mail." I grabbed the invitation.

The invitation was green and yellow. COME TO MY PARTY was printed in green on the side of a little wagon that had yellow wheels. On the inside of the invitation the date and time were filled in. The party was on a Saturday night. It didn't make any difference which Saturday night it was because I had empty Saturday nights lined up for the next two years.

"Well, I guess the best things in life really *are* free," said Mom. "You should see how happy you look."

"Who's Melissa Gertz?" asked Dad.

"She's this really stuck-up girl in Mitch's class. All the kids in that family are stuck-up."

"Really, Lynda, it's up to your brother whether he wants to go to Melissa's party," said Mom. "Let's leave it at that. We have all these letters to go through tonight."

I wasn't going to tell Lynda, but I was beginning to think the same thing. Before the sweepstakes, I would have given anything for an invitation from Melissa Gertz. For *anything* from Melissa Gertz. But now I wasn't so sure anymore. Still, this was just what I had hoped for—real attention from Melissa.

The next letter was from a man who wanted me to air-condition his worm farm.

· 11 ·

The minute I said yes to Melissa I wished I
had said no. She started to get all gushy. "Oh
goody, terrific," she said. "You can tell us all
about your contest. Can you autograph the
invitation I sent you and give it back to me?"

"Uh, well . . . ."

"Do you use a special pen when you give
autographs?"

"Uh, Melissa, why didn't you talk to me before or smile or something?"

"Well, you know, it's hard to talk to everybody."

Mr. Devon was about to start the class, so we stopped talking. I wondered if Melissa was going to serve avocado sandwiches at her party. I wondered how I could get out of going to her party. I couldn't.

"Psst!"

Melissa was trying to get my attention. She handed me a folded piece of paper.

I opened it. She had written a poem.

You've got a new friend
Her name is Melissa
She won't turn away
If you try to kiss her.

Oh, no! This couldn't be happening to me.

After class I rushed right out of the room. I saw Newton in the hallway. I ran to catch up with him. "Hey, Newton, don't you want to get together?"

"You're busy," said Newton. "Everybody knows you're busy."

Newton walked away. "But, Newt . . . ." I said after him. I was beginning to miss his phone calls. They had been part of my regular life, not this crazy life where strangers kept calling. I never thought I'd miss pesty Newton.

I walked home with Roseanne. Every time I saw her I thought about my promise. If only she'd say something about it! Did she forget about the promise or was she waiting for *me* to bring it up?

"Are you going to Melissa's party?" I asked.

"You know I'm not one of Melissa's crowd."

"I'm not either, but she invited me. So I thought maybe she invited you."

"I'm not rich or famous," said Roseanne.

"What does that mean?"

"You know how Melissa is. She only talks to the great ones."

"Maybe she's nicer than you think."

"No. I've thought about it, and she isn't. When did she invite *you*? Before or after?"

"Before or after what?"

"You know what I mean."

First Newton, then her. I hoped more trouble wasn't ahead. I had a telephone call to make as soon as I got home.

"May I speak to Sergeant Grimes, please?

"Hi, Sergeant Grimes. This is Mitchell Dartmouth. I'm calling about Lambykins. Did you find his owner?"

"Yes and no."

I waited.

"Yes, we found out the owner's name. The dog belongs to a Mrs. Dementia Landsdorf and she lives on Oakdale Street. But, no, we haven't actually found her. She doesn't answer her telephone, and she doesn't answer her door. We've been out to her house a few times, but no one was home. We left notes. We also spoke to neighbors. They said that Mrs. Landsdorf does live there. She just doesn't answer her door. We left messages with the neighbors, too."

"So you still have Lambykins?"

"He's at the Humane Society."

"But they could destroy him!"

"No, we told them we're in the midst of contacting his owner."

"Do you suppose someone might come along and want to adopt him?"

"Are you kidding? How many truly insane people do you think there are in this world?"

"All we need is one."

"Well, I'll let you know if one shows up."

"Don't forget." I *had* to do something for Lambykins! It was my fault that he didn't have a home.

I added a Doberman pinscher to my list of sweepstakes troubles.

·12·

"What are we going to do with one hundred and thirty-five thousand dollars?" asked Dad.

We were all sitting around the living room after supper. The telephone receiver was off the hook.

"What happened to the two hundred and fifty thousand?" asked Lynda.

"Taxes happened to it," said Mom. "The accountant says this is what we have left."

Actually we didn't have one hundred and thirty-five thousand dollars left. Mom had already ordered about one hundred dollars worth of subscriptions to financial magazines.

Dad said, "First I think we should pay off the loan on the car."

"The car?" I said. "With my money?"

"Well, Mitchell, you ride in the car, don't you?"

"Okay," I said. "How much?"

Mom and Dad both had pencils and paper. "Approximately four thousand dollars," said Dad.

"Next," he said, "let's think about the mortgage on the house."

"I want to move to a rich neighborhood," said Lynda.

"Mortgages are boring," I said. "Let's do something that's fun with the money."

"Wait," said Dad. "First come the practical things. Like your education."

"I'm getting an education right now," I said.

"I'm talking about college and graduate school or professional school," said Dad.

"Ho hum."

"Mom and I plan to put away fifty thousand dollars for your education."

"What about *my* education?" asked Lynda. "I want to be a veterinarian."

"We're coming to that," said Dad. "Your mother and I were prepared to spend equally for your education and Mitchell's. But now that Mitchell is somewhat rich . . . ."

"*Somewhat?*" said Lynda.

"Your mother and I think that we should pay for your education, Lynda, and Mitchell should pay for his own. We think that's both fair and unfair but we don't know any way around it."

"Mitch could pay for my education," said Lynda.

"Are we talking about one hundred thousand dollars of my money?" I asked.

"Well, Lynda has a career goal, and that's going to cost money," said Dad. "You should have a goal, too, Mitchell. Don't you want to be something?"

"I already am something."

"I mean don't you want a career when you grow up?"

"An astronaut is a fine choice," said Mom. "You love to travel, Mitchell."

"I don't want to be an astronaut," I said. "I have a goal, but you won't like it. I want to run sweepstakes contests."

"Oh, you mean a business executive. Excellent," said Dad. "Then it's settled. The money will be put aside so that you can attend college and a professional business school afterwards."

"One of my financial magazines says Stanford is the best," said Mom. "Is Stanford all right with you, Mitchell?"

"If it's all right with Stanford," I said.

"We won't be moving to a rich neighborhood, will we," said Lynda. "Haven't you just spent most of the money?"

"Not if I don't educate you," I said.

Dad said, "Let's just think about this for a while. We don't have to decide tonight, but as a family we should consider what's best for all of us."

"But I want to do *some* fun things with my money," I said. "So far we haven't talked about one fun thing."

"Well, if you decide—and it *is* your decision, Mitchell—to pay for Lynda's education, and if we pay off the car and our taxes, we'll have about thirty thousand dollars left. And you know our roof looks pretty bad." I saw Dad write down the word roof.

"Our roof? I don't care about our roof," I said.

"Well, Mitchell, you would if it fell down on you."

Mom spoke up. "We could get a roof you'd be *proud* of, Mitchell. The latest look is to have one or more turrets. Sort of a medieval theme. I saw it in one of my magazines. We'd have the only house in the neighborhood that looks like a castle."

"Oh, great!" Lynda moaned.

"You can fly your own flag up there," said

Mom. "With the family coat of arms embroidered on it."

"What family coat of arms?" I asked.

"That's another thing I saw in my magazines. You can get your *own* family coat of arms designed for less than six hundred dollars. That is, if you act within the next thirty days. After that the price goes up to a thousand."

Mom took off her watch, jacket and shoes. "The thought of having my own coat of arms is so exciting!"

"I want to go to California," I said. "I want to see the Pacific Ocean. I want a huge color TV set just for myself. I want . . . ."

"Mitchell, first we take care of our needs and then we take care of our wants," said Dad.

"But . . . ."

"Tell you what, Mitchell. We'll take you along when we go to see a lawyer. We'll discuss everything with him. How's that?"

"It stinks."

I wanted to say, "Okay, you big spenders, now hear this: I promised Roseanne Rich $125,000. And a promise is a promise."

Lynda spoke up and my brave moment passed. "I don't like discussions where Mitch and I lose because we're too young to win."

"Me too," I said.

I wished I could buy a rich neighborhood and a horse for Lynda.

· 13 ·

The lawyer, Blake Reynolds IV, looked as if *he* had won $250,000 and had spent it all on his office. His desk was long enough to seat six people without their knees bumping. It was on a platform, which made it a little higher up than we were.

Mr. Reynolds was surrounded by things that made him look smart: books, diplomas, papers. He looked as if he had been sitting behind that desk all his life, getting smarter and richer every minute. He charged by the *minute*.

"Don't say anything extra to him," Dad told

me. "Say hi, but that's it. Got it? One word. One syllable. Just remember that a sentence could cost a dollar."

Mr. Reynolds' fee was actually one hundred and twenty dollars an hour, but Dad said we'd have to think of it as two dollars each minute or we'd talk too much.

Mr. Reynolds was a member of a big law firm in New York City. His name was fourth down in the list of names of the firm. The first two names were dead. After we had shaken hands with him and sat down, he turned to me and asked, "Well, Mitchell, how does it feel to win $250,000?"

"Fine."

Mom and Dad nodded approvingly.

Mr. Reynolds studied some papers on his desk. Then he said to my parents, "I understand that Mitchell actually entered the contest but the sweepstakes prize was awarded in your names."

"Yes," said Mom.

Mr. Reynolds turned back to me. "How do you feel about that, Mitchell?"

"Fine."

Mom and Dad nodded again.

Then I said, "Why couldn't they have trusted me with the money?"

Mom made a face at me. She was mouthing "two dollars a minute."

"Who are *they*?" asked Mr. Reynolds. "Your parents or the sweepstakes sponsors?"

"Well, everybody."

My father spoke up. "We want to put the money away for Mitchell. A trust fund. Something where he can't touch the principal till he's forty-five or fifty."

"Forty-five or fifty?" I was gasping.

"Mitchell," said my father, "if we gave it to you in one lump sum at age twenty-one, it might be gone by twenty-two."

"That stinks!"

We were paying Mr. Reynolds two dollars a minute to watch us fight.

Mom said, "Let's *listen* to Mr. Reynolds."

Mom reached down and took off her right shoe. Then she removed her scarf, a pin, and her watch.

"Well," said Mr. Reynolds, "although we think of twenty-one as the beginning of maturity, Mitchell should be able to benefit from the use of those funds earlier should the need arise. Of course, tax considerations will . . . ."

Mr. Reynold's buzzer sounded.

"Excuse me," he said.

Mr. Reynolds started to talk to somebody on the phone. On our two dollars a minute. Mom was dying. I knew she was getting hot. She took off her other shoe and her belt. She was feeling her stockings.

Mr. Reynolds was making dinner plans with his wife. Before they were through, our family had paid for the entire meal.

Mr. Reynolds turned back to us. "Sorry for the interruption," he said.

He wasn't half as sorry as Mom.

"Mitchell's interests must be protected," he said. "That's what we all want, isn't it?"

"Fine," Mom, Dad, and I said all at the same time.

Mom turned to me. "Mitchell, now that you know Mr. Reynolds will be representing *your* interests—do you think you could step out and get me some aspirin? I saw a drugstore about twenty blocks from here."

I was glad to get out of there. I did Mom a favor and took half an hour to buy the aspirin. You might say that was a sixty-dollar favor.

· 14 ·

I was now calling Sergeant Grimes about twice a day.

"Nothing has happened in the last five minutes," he said early one morning.

I think that was his way of telling me I was calling too much. He sounded beat.

"Don't the police have ways of getting to a person? I mean, there must be something official you can do to get hold of Mrs. Landsdorf."

"Sure, there are things we can do. But we don't like to frighten a poor old woman. Her neighbors are trying to contact her. That's what we're waiting on right now. Maybe your insane stranger might show up to adopt Lambykins. Keep that thought. Goodby."

I sat by the telephone. I was getting as tired of calling Sergeant Grimes as he was of hearing from me. I picked up the receiver and called him again.

"Look, son," he said. "I admire tenacity. I really do. And you've got it. But you've got too much of it. Have you ever heard of obscene phone calls? Your calls are beginning to qualify."

"No, this call is different. I want Mrs. Landsdorf's address. You said Oakdale Street. Could you give me the number?"

"What for?"

"Look, I know policemen like to take in information, and not give it out. But I thought I'd try to see Mrs. Landsdorf."

"I don't know, sonny. She's on the weird side. The house she's living in is falling down. And I heard barking and yelping inside. I haven't met her but I'd say she's one of your basic eccentrics."

"The address. Please."

"Listen, you're a good kid. I'll give you the address if you promise to tell your parents what you're planning to do."

The word *promise* wasn't my all-time favorite word. I promised.

I wrote down 12 Oakdale Street. If I had to call Sergeant Grimes back for it, he might become violent.

After school I told my mother I was going to Oakdale Street to look for Lambykins's owner. "That's not the best neighborhood," she said. "It's old."

"What's wrong with old?"

"Just be careful. What if she's got more Lambykinses around? What if she breeds them?"

"Sergeant Grimes would have told me."

"Well, all right. But don't hang around there too long. She probably has bite marks all over her body."

Mrs. Landsdorf's house was easy to find. It was the worst house on the street. It made ours look like a palace. Rotting steps, peeling paint, and a hundred different kind of weeds. I walked up the steps. I heard barking inside. I saw a doorbell and I rang it. It worked. More barking.

The door opened! A lady peered out. She looked like her house. In need of things. Everything about her looked like it could be better. Her clothes. Her hair. She looked older than my mother and younger than my grandmother.

She opened the door wider and five Doberman pinschers ran out! There were more inside. I could hear them barking. I was terrified. So this was where my life was going to end!

"They're all friendly," said the woman. "They're one big family. Brothers and sisters, mothers and fathers, aunts and uncles. I started with two or three and the family just grew and grew."

"I already met one of the family," I said. "I'm Mitchell Dartmouth. You gave me Lambykins."

"Come in," she said, and she smiled. She let me and the five dogs into the house. The inside of her house was as bad as the outside. And I couldn't believe all the dogs! I started to count them under my breath.

The woman noticed. "There are seventeen," she said. Then she said to me, "Sit!"

She sounded like a dog owner. Sometimes they say sit instead of sit down.

"I'm Dementia Landsdorf," she said. "Welcome to Landsdorf Landing. That is, it *used* to be called Landsdorf Landing when I had my boardinghouse. But my boarders got scared away."

"By the dogs?"

"The dogs have good manners. Notice that they're not attacking you. But it's hard to keep up a boardinghouse and a family of dogs. As the dogs came and the roof went, my boarders departed."

Mrs. Landsdorf went into her kitchen. She

came back with a pitcher of something. "Would you like a protein drink? I make it for my dogs."

"No, that's okay."

She poured the drink into bowls that were scattered around the place. Each bowl had a different dog's name on it. Maybe they could read.

"Would you like some bone-shaped cookies? I bake them for my dogs, but humans can eat them, too. At least I think so."

"I'm not very hungry." I raised my voice. It was hard to talk with all the dogs yelping. "Uh, first I want to thank you for giving up Lambykins. Unfortunately I can't keep him. So I'd like to give your generous gift back to you. In fact, the police have been around trying to contact you about it."

"Oh, I know that. I peek through my curtains. But I didn't answer the door. For you I answered the door."

Mrs. Landsdorf said that as if she had given me a great compliment.

"The police don't understand dogs," she

said. "My dogs are smarter than people. Listen, my dogs could run that police department." Mrs. Landsdorf walked around and patted each and every dog. She called them dearie and sweetie and honeycake.

"Want to see a trick?" she asked. "One of my dogs can put his teeth on your clothes but *not* bite through. You *think* he's going to but he isn't!"

"Well, let's wait on that. You see, I came for the same reason as the police. To give Lambykins back to you. He's at the animal shelter right now. We wouldn't want anything to happen to him, would we?"

Mrs. Landsdorf suddenly looked sad. "No," she said.

"It's not that we don't appreciate your gift. I mean, everybody else seems to be trying to take my money away. At least you *gave* me something."

"No, I didn't. I'm as bad as the others. I couldn't afford to keep Lambykins any longer. He's my youngest dog. I can't feed any more dogs. I was already cutting down on his meals. So I gave him to you to take care of. Is there a worse present than a starving Doberman pinscher?"

"How about a boa constrictor who hasn't had a hug in a long time?"

Mrs. Landsdorf smiled. "He *is* a good guard dog. With a little training he'd protect you from absolutely everything."

"Don't you miss him?"

"You bet I miss him. But I hardly have enough food for myself and the other dogs."

"Don't you have any money?"

"Enough."

"Enough for what?"

"Enough to get by if I could get this house fixed up. I can't take in boarders anymore until the roof is repaired. It's dangerous."

"How much money would it take to fix up the roof?"

"More than I've got."

I couldn't think of anything else to say. So I said, "Well, I guess I'll be going."

"What about Lambykins? You own him now. Take care of him."

On the way home I wondered if Thelma Scrinch of New South Wales, Australia, would consider taking in a living pet for under thirty thousand dollars.

·15·

"I need five hundred dollars."

"For what?" asked my mother.

"I just need it. Sort of for a charity."

"Did one of those letters get to you?"

"This is legitimate."

"I'll have to talk to your father."

"*I* won the money. I can spend a little bit of it if I want to."

"You're only eleven, Mitchell. And five hundred dollars isn't a little bit of money. You should tell your father and me what you want it for."

"It's a secret. So just say yes. I won't nag you anymore if you do."

"Well, it *is* your money. But please reconsider."

"I'll take it in five one hundred dollar bills."

"That's cash!" my mother exclaimed.

"It sure is. Don't you think I deserve it for winning the contest and making us rich?"

"Well, you *do* deserve it. I'm not the kind of mother who would deprive a child of what he *deserves*."

"Good."

"I really try to be a devoted mother. I gave up the turrets and the coat of arms . . . ."

"Please. Just the five hundred bucks."

"What a little entrepreneur you've become, Mitchell."

The next day my mother came back from the bank with five one hundred dollar bills—the first I'd seen of any of the money I won. The bills looked new and clean. She handed them to me with a sigh.

I went to my room, closed the door, put the money in an envelope, sealed it, and addressed it to Mrs. Dementia Landsdorf at 12 Oakdale Street.

I didn't know if Mrs. Landsdorf would accept charity. But what could she do with a surprise gift that had no name on it? She might suspect it was from me, but she wouldn't have any proof. I hoped that the money was enough to repair her roof so her boarders would come back and pay her and she could afford to keep her dogs and take back Lambykins.

Ten minutes after I mailed the envelope, I picked up one of the financial magazines that were littering the house. I started to read it. There was an article in it on financial con games. "The most successful con games," the article said, "are those in which the person who gets conned is manipulated into a position where he or she becomes terribly anxious to part with his or her money. No one begs or even asks for it. If done correctly, the person can't wait to give the con artist vast sums of money."

I thought about Dementia Landsdorf. I

tracked her down. She didn't make it easy to find her but she didn't make it hard. The dog license was available for the police department to trace. But she didn't open her door for the police. She opened it for me. Rich Mitch. Did she really give me the dog just so I could feed it?

Yikes! After turning down the nephew of a fat lady who might not be fat, a starving boy who wasn't starving and wasn't a boy, the pet lady from Australia, the air-conditioned worm person and loads of others, had I finally been taken?

·16·

My life was a mess. I felt uncomfortable around my best friend Roseanne. Melissa was writing more and more sappy poems to me. Newton's trademark had become the weak wave. That's all I got from him. Not even one telephone call. My phone wasn't anywhere near as busy as it had been after the contest news broke.

My parents were trying very hard to remember that it was *my* money that had taken over their lives. Mom interviewed several roofers and she bought a huge oil painting of a spinach garden. Dad bought a new suit and a pair of eighty-five-dollar shoes. We now owned our car free and clear. Lynda had her hair styled by Ormanne. She hardly ever insulted me any more. That was the high spot of my life.

The low spot was the thing with Dementia Landsdorf, because it reminded me of how stupid I was. I figured that she hung out part-time in that ramshackle house and rented those dogs just to entice suckers like me. The rest of the time she wore beautiful clothes and lived in a beautiful house toward which I had contributed five hundred dollars.

I called Sergeant Grimes a couple of days after I sent out the money. What if, by some miracle, I was wrong and Mrs. Landsdorf had claimed her dog now that she had money.

This time I didn't get straight through to Sergeant Grimes. Someone asked, "Who is calling Sergeant Grimes?"

"Mitchell Dartmouth."

"Sergeant Grimes is on assignment."

"Where?"

"Pakistan."

"Oh."

"Is this about Lambykins Landsdorf?"

"Yes."

"No progress. Also, we've been informed by the Humane Society that Lambykins cannot be boarded much longer without compensation. 'Boarding a bruiser like that costs money.' That's a direct quote from them."

"Thank you. When will Sergeant Grimes be back so that I can talk to him personally?"

"Never."

"That's what I thought."

It was a depressing phone call. I could just see Sergeant Grimes shaking the hand of the guy who'd told me about his assignment in Pakistan. And I saw Dementia Landsdorf congratulating herself on her latest successful caper. She was blowing kisses at my five hundred dollars while she looked over travel folders for her trip around the world.

I decided to go back to Oakdale Street and try to get my five hundred dollars back. That wouldn't be easy. I could probably take it away from her if she had it on her, but over-powering an old lady didn't seem like the best idea. Trying to talk her out of it probably wouldn't work either. She was too slick for me. All I could do was tell her off.

I was all steamed up by the time I got to Oakdale Street. What if she wasn't there and I got all steamed up for nothing. This was only her make-believe poverty house, not her home. I heard pounding sounds as I got near the house. There were two guys in jeans working on the roof! She *was* having her roof fixed. I ran up the steps and rang the bell. She opened the door right away. She hugged me as her dogs ran out. "You gave me the five hundred dollars, didn't you. How can I ever thank you!"

I walked in. Mrs. Landsdorf kept on talking. "I got these two nice young men to work on my roof. Some day they're going to fix the rest of the house. But two of my former boarders are coming back next month. They said they don't mind living in an ugly house in

Dog City but they do mind living under a collapsing roof. Once they pay me, I'll have enough money to bring Lambykins back home. Could you take care of him for just one month?"

"Can I sit down?" I asked. "I want to think about this."

"My house is your house," said Mrs. Landsdorf. "Although I'm sure you wouldn't want it."

This *couldn't* be a con game. The guys were up there fixing the roof. And Mrs. Landsdorf wasn't hinting that she needed more money.

She acted as if her problem was solved, and that she could take care of Lambykins. But five hundred dollars wouldn't fix the roof permanently. I knew that from listening to the roof guys who talked with Mom. Before long, Mrs. Landsdorf would be out of money again.

"The only problem left is what to do about Lambykins for the month," said Mrs. Landsdorf.

"I'll take care of that."

"You will? Then I don't have to worry about Lambykins?"

"No, I do." I stood up. "I'll take care of everything," I said.

"But aren't you rather young to take care of everything, as you put it?"

"Yeah."

I walked home slowly. I had just made another promise. To take care of Lambykins for a month. This could be more expensive than the promise I made to Roseanne. It could cost me my life.

·17·

"Rog Hemingway, please," I said for the third time as I got connected to one person after another at Dazzle Detergent. I was getting tired of holding the telephone receiver. And I was afraid I'd be told that Rog was on assignment in Pakistan.

"Rog Hemingway here."

At last! "Rog, this is Mitchell Dartmouth." My voice was a little shaky.

"Hey, how goes it, Mitchell?"

"Okay. How're things with you and Dazzle?"

"Couldn't be better."

"Good. I'm calling because I need to go on national television."

"You *were* on national television," said Rog.

"Yeah. I'd like to do it again."

"Wouldn't everybody," said Rog. "What I mean is, Mitchell, as they say in show biz, I think you've peaked."

"Peaked?"

"No offense, Mitchell. But the public wants fresh faces. You won the sweepstakes, when was it, three, four weeks ago. In television that's a *very* long time."

"I thought, like, once you're on, you get more and more popular."

"Sometimes that happens. Sometimes it doesn't. Frankly I thought we'd be flooded with requests for your appearance, but it's been a little, uh, thin. Disappointing. Even your parrot peaked quickly. Tell me, why do you suddenly want to go on TV?"

"Because I gave five hundred dollars to this lady who isn't one of your basic eccentrics or a

106

con artist and she lives in this crumbly old house and she needs money so she can fix her roof and take in boarders so she can afford to feed her monster dog."

"Well, Mitchell, this is definitely a fresh slant. I'll see what I can do. Call you back."

Rog was off the phone before I could say another word.

Al called back four hours later. "Rog is tied up," he said. "So I'll tell you the good news. We weren't able to book you, but we did get a spot for your lady friend on the *Isn't It Fantastic* show."

"I've never heard of it."

"That's because it's new. It premieres this Saturday night. They're looking for fresh talent."

"This isn't a haircut and new clothes show, is it?"

"Oh, no. This show digs deeply into the human condition. No light stuff. It's perfect for your needy lady. She'll have a chance to win valuable prizes."

As soon as Al hung up, I called the Humane Society. For nine dollars a day I could board Lambykins. Great! What was nine dollars a day to a rich guy like me.

·18·

"I need two hundred and seventy dollars."

My mother immediately started to take off her clothes. "Mitchell, these requests are upsetting me. Why do you need this money?"

"Actually I need only nine dollars a day for a month. That's not so bad, is it?"

"It's not a minor sum, Mitchell. It could purchase a set of personalized swans to put on our front lawn."

"Personalized swans?"

"Yes. Four swans, each with a name of a member of our family. Your father would be the biggest swan, then I come next . . . ."

"I don't want to be a swan."

"I can't break up the set."

"If I agree to be a swan, can I have the two hundred and seventy dollars?"

"I'm afraid not, Mitchell. This is getting to be a habit, a trend. Success in extracting money from people only encourages more requests. Mitchell, at this point, for your own sake, you desperately need to fail. Request denied."

"Then I'm not going to be a swan."

"Dumb Dennis is a member of our family. Perhaps I could use his name."

I went outside. I had done the best I could. I had agreed to be a swan. But I still couldn't get the money to take care of Lambykins for a month. There was only one thing left to do.

Two hours later I was back in the house again. My mother had all of her clothes on. Maybe she was in a good mood.

"He's kind and smart and friendly and he's outside," I said to my mother.

"Who?"

"Lambykins Landsdorf."

"The name sounds familiar. Is he a new friend of yours?"

"You've got it," I said. "And a friend of yours, too."

"Well, you and I don't always agree on everything, but when it comes to your friends, I'm very open-minded. Remember that little girl who threw bricks. . . ."

"This friend doesn't throw bricks."

"Good. You should stick to your own type."

"So can I bring him in?"

"As I said, Mitchell, the welcome mat is always there for your friends."

I went outside and brought in Lambykins on his leash.

My mother took one look at him and screamed, "It's that monster! Run, Mitchell, run!"

She grabbed me and pulled me away from Lambykins.

"You don't have to run, Mom. He's harmless. He just looks ugly and sounds ugly."

"And bites ugly," said Mom.

"Mrs. Landsdorf, that's his owner, says he doesn't bite."

Mom was still pulling me. "We'll discuss this outside, Mitchell."

She pulled me out of the house and closed the door behind her. "Now, Mitchell, we got rid of this dog once. This *is* the same dog, isn't it? I never forget teeth. You know that. Why do we have this dog the second time when we didn't want it the first time?"

"Because Mrs. Landsdorf owns seventeen other dogs. And she can't afford to feed them all, and her boarders left. The boarders paid rent. The dogs don't. They just eat. So I'm taking Lambykins for a month. Mrs. Landsdorf is going on TV and she's getting rich, I think."

"I don't understand, and I don't want to."

Mom looked at me. Suddenly she was calm. "Are you out of your mind?" she asked.

She didn't wait for an answer. "I'm going to call that Sergeant whatever his name is," she said, "and tell him to pick up this dog."

"Sergeant Grimes is on assignment in

Pakistan. Look, how about this? We'll keep Lambykins for the month unless he bites somebody."

Mom started to take off her clothes.

"Mrs. Landsdorf said that Lambykins loves to be with people. He likes people so much that he gets sad and lonely without them."

Mom kept taking off her clothes. We were outside in broad daylight.

"This is just about a perfect dog, Mom. Except when he's left alone. But that's his only fault."

My mother stopped. "What did you say?"

"I said he gets sad and lonely without people. A lot of dogs are like that. If you leave them alone they tear around the house and dig their claws into walls and pull down drapes and . . . ."

I heard crashing sounds coming from inside the house. Mom and I turned and looked through our big front window. There was Lambykins trying desperately to get out. He was leaping against the window pane.

"No!" cried Mom.

We ran inside. The kitchen was a wreck!

The curtains were torn to shreds. Dishes were in pieces on the floor. There were scratch marks on the refrigerator. Plants were uprooted.

"I do *not* want to know what he did to the living room," said Mom. "You look, but don't tell me. Remember, I do not want to know."

I went into the living room. The piano had a long gash in it. I looked at the ripped sofa and remembered how much Mom had wanted a new one anyway. Well, she was certainly going to get one now. I would have to buy it for her.

Lambykins came leaping up to me and licked me. He wasn't lonely anymore.

Mom was yelling, "How is it in there? I don't want to know, but tell me!"

I yelled back. "No problem! I'll pay for the new sofa and new piano. And for the rug cleaning."

Mom's shriek was so loud that even Lambykins jumped.

114

· 19 ·

I decided to wear my new suit to Melissa's party. This was the suit that was bought before the eyes of millions of the viewing public, as Rog had described it. I thought about going back to Ormanne for a haircut. But the day before the party I went to my three-dollar barber. He was so excited to get me back after my fifty-dollar haircut that he cut off too much. My hair stuck up like splinters. Then I remembered how Ormanne had cut off a lot but made it look like I'd grown more.

"Horrors!" Mom said when I got home.

"I want to go to Ormanne," I said.

"Fifty dollars for a haircut. Ridiculous!" said Mom.

"I'd just be spending some of *my* money," I said. "What have I gotten so far? I have some new clothes that Dazzle Detergent paid for and I've redecorated the living room."

"Aren't you forgetting that you spent five hundred dollars on some mysterious project?"

"Oh, that."

I kept my splinters haircut.

Melissa lives eight blocks away. Mom and Dad drove me over there. They were going out for the night.

"Have a good time," Dad said as I got out of the car.

A good time! I just wanted to get the party over with.

Melissa's house was lit up on the inside and the outside. I rang the bell. Melissa answered it. "Well hi, famous person," she said.

I walked in. There were a lot of kids standing around. I didn't really know anyone. Melissa started quizzing me right away. "Tell us all about being on television, Mitch. Did they put makeup on your face? Did they tell you what to say? Is that your famous haircut?" Melissa was staring at my hair. "No, I guess it isn't," she said.

I couldn't get any chips or soda because kids kept asking me questions.

I may have peaked with the TV viewing public, but Melissa and her crowd were just getting started. I was the big attraction at the party. I had never been so popular.

So this was what it was like at the top. It was like Lambykins drooling over a piece of raw liver the way these kids were hanging all over me. Not one of them had ever even spoken to me before. They were starting to remind me of the letter writers. Melissa and her friends weren't after my money, but they wanted to be connected with me in some way. I was the right person to know.

I didn't want to stick around. I found myself

wondering what Roseanne was doing tonight, and if she was mad about the $125,000 I still owed her. What was she waiting for? Could she have forgotten? If I said anything, she'd *know* I owed her the money.

Melissa was holding up a piece of paper. "Attention! Attention!" she said. "I want to read a poem I wrote in honor of Mitch."

"I have to leave," I said.

"So soon? You just got here."

"I just remembered I have some sweep-stakes business to take care of. There's big money involved. It's hard to explain. The price of fame, you know. These things do come up." I hated to hear myself talking like that. But it worked.

Melissa clapped her hands. "Listen, everybody. Mitch has to dash off. Sweepstakes business."

"Thanks for everything, Melissa," I said.

I walked out as Melissa started to read,

Mitchell Dartmouth is a star
Twinkling brightly from afar . . .

Lights were on in Roseanne's house when I got there. I knew she wasn't having a party, but I hoped she didn't have company. I knocked quietly on the door.

Roseanne answered the door. "Hello, stranger. What are you doing here? You're all dressed up."

"I went to Melissa's party and left. Can I come in?"

Roseanne looked puzzled. "Okay," she said.

Roseanne's parents were in the living room, so we went into the kitchen. We sat down at the table. I've sat there a lot. But not lately.

I spoke fast. "Roseanne, I'm sorry."

"About what?"

"About not, well, I haven't been as good a friend, well, there's something . . . ."

I made myself say it.

"Roseanne, I promised you half of my DAZZLE-RAMA SWEEPSTAKES prize if I won. I won. So I *owe* you $125,000."

"You've got to be kidding."

"Don't you remember? I was dropping my entry into the mailbox on the way to school."

"Sure, I remember you were kidding about it."

"But I *promised*."

"Mitch, it was just a joke to get me off your back. You didn't mean it."

"But I think it was an oral contract. I read about them in one of my mother's financial magazines. Somebody built an empire on one."

121

"Look, Mitch, did I ever even hint that you owed me the money?"

"No. I've been waiting for the ax to fall. I've been, well, hoping you forgot about the promise. I admit it."

"I remembered it as a joke. Let's leave it at that. What happened to your hair?"

"How about another subject?"

"Want to stick around and watch TV? There's a new show on, *Isn't It Fantastic.* It's just starting tonight."

I went into the living room with Roseanne. Her parents were watching TV.

"It's on," Roseanne whispered. We sat down on the floor.

I was so glad to be friends with Roseanne again that I hardly even watched all the weirdos who were parading across the TV screen on *Isn't It Fantastic.* Then it hit me. In a few weeks Mrs. Landsdorf would be on that show. Tonight's main feature was a man who married a gorilla. There she was in her apron in their kitchen, standing over a stove, cooking. Next, a woman who slept on her head on top of a mountain had a perfectly logical explanation for doing it. And a lady who ran a clinic for nasal congestion sufferers brought out five smiling patients she cured by a diet of pickle and sauerkraut juice.

I had thought that getting Mrs. Landsdorf on the show would solve all her problems. Maybe I hadn't done her a favor.

· 20 ·

I told the animal-shelter people that Lambykins's owner was going on a national TV show and that Lambykins would soon be famous. They wouldn't want anything to happen to a dog who was about to become famous, would they?

They didn't believe me. But then I told them the name of the show and when to watch it. *"Isn't It Fantastic,"* I said. "Look for Mrs. Dementia Landsdorf."

"Isn't It Fantastic? Is that the show that had a man who said he was descended from a dan-

delion? He traced his evolution from weed to person."

"That's it," I said. "So just hold on to Lamb-ykins."

Lynda and my parents went out the night *Isn't It Fantastic* had Mrs. Landsdorf for a guest. I was glad about that. I wanted Mrs. Landsdorf to win lots of prizes, but I didn't want anyone to see her do it. I kept thinking that maybe I shouldn't have put her on the show. I especially felt that way when I turned on my television set and saw Mrs. Landsdorf seated beside a family that had spent an entire week inside a huge chicken costume. They were still in it. She was staring at the chicken family and feeling their costume with her fingers.

The host of the program, Rap Sprintfellow, was saying, "And here's our third fantastic contestant, Dr. Egram Tamrahs, the acclaimed author of *Your Toenails and You*. This book explains why you should never—and I mean *never*—cut your toenails. It goes against nature."

Rap held up a book that had a huge toenail on the cover.

A man hobbled out on crutches. No wonder. His toenails must have been a foot long! He sat down on the other side of Mrs. Landsdorf. She leaned over and carefully examined his feet.

Rap said, "And now I'm going to briefly interview the contestants before they compete for our fantastic prizes. First Mrs. Dementia Landsdorf."

Mrs. Landsdorf started to talk about her dogs. "I give them love and attention and a mother's care," she said. "There is no place on earth where a dog gets as much affection as at Landsdorf's Landing. But the dogs are hungry. I don't have enough money to feed them decent meals."

"How did you get so many hungry canine mouths to feed?" Rap asked cheerfully.

"One dog led to another. I used to run a boardinghouse. But as the dogs came, the boarders left."

Rap smiled into the camera. *"Isn't it fantastic,* Mr. and Mrs. America?"

"Cluck!"

One of the chicken people sitting beside Mrs. Landsdorf clucked. Then he clucked again. "Cluck! Cluck!"

Mrs. Landsdorf was mad. She turned to the chicken person and tugged his costume. "Stop that! This is serious."

"Cluck!"

Rap's smile faded. But he recovered quickly. "Dogs and chickens don't always get along together," he smiled. "Well then, I want to thank Mrs. Dementia Landsdorf for giving us yet another reason for saying ISN'T IT FANTASTIC! And after our commercial we'll take a peek into the barnyard caper of a family that refused to . . . *chicken out!"*

The commercial went on.

I switched off the set. I couldn't stand another minute of that program. Still, I had to see if Mrs. Landsdorf won the prizes.

I turned the set back on.

Rap was saying, "And now our contestants will compete for prizes. Our Fantast-O-Meter will record the responses of our studio audience and select the winner. First, the chicken family will dance THE COOP."

"I don't want to do that dumb dance!" a boy called from inside the chicken.

"It's not dumb!" another voice said inside the chicken.

Suddenly the chicken family started to fight. Legs and wings moved up and down frantically. I looked closer. Two parents and about five kids were inside the suit. The parts operated on wires and levers and stuff. A drumstick broke. Fake feathers flew off. Now the chicken was on its back. One kid yelled, "I'll get you!" A phony egg rolled across the stage. The chicken collapsed.

"What a fowl blow, ha ha!" said Rap. "We'll now register the response of our studio audience on our Fantast-O-Meter."

"No! We're supposed to be doing a dance," Mom Chicken called from inside the suit.

The Fantast-O-Meter was already going wild. It looked like an outer-space thermometer. "Ninety-eight out of a possible one hundred!" said Rap.

Rap turned to the toenails man. "And now for his entry into the competition, Dr. Tamrahs will *walk*!"

Dr. Tamrahs stood up and walked back and forth without his crutches. Click. Click. Click. His toenails sounded like a musical instrument that had gone out of tune.

The audience cheered and the Fantast-O-Meter went crazy.

"A very respectable ninety-two!" said Rap. "The chickens are leading by six points. And now Mrs. Landsdorf will try to top that with her monologue."

Mrs. Landsdorf got up. "I want to talk about needy dogs," she said. "Doberman pinschers eat so much, you know. And I have so many of them. . . ."

Rap looked distressed. "Excuse me, Mrs. Landsdorf, but could you *imitate* a dog?"

The audience whistled.

"But I have a real problem . . . ."

"Of course," said Rap. "And now we are all aware of it. How about a big hand from the audience for Mrs. Dementia Landsdorf!"

Mrs. Landsdorf got a small hand. The Fantast-O-Meter hardly moved.

The chicken family won the prizes. A one-way bus ticket to El Paso, Texas, fifty deluxe TV dinners, and a framed certificate naming them as a winner on *Isn't It Fantastic*.

I turned off the TV set and kept it off.

· 21 ·

"Mitchell?"

Mrs. Landsdorf was telephoning me. It was two days after the TV show.

"Oh, hi, Mrs. Landsdorf. I've, uh, been thinking about visiting you and hoping you won't set your dogs on me because I got you on that terrible TV show. . . ."

"*Terrible* TV show? It's the tops, that's what it is!"

"*What?*"

"You must come right over to celebrate."

"Celebrate what?"

"You'll see."

"Are your dogs particularly hungry or vicious today?"

"Mitchell, nobody's going to hurt you. Now rush right over."

I took my time walking to Mrs. Landsdorf's house. I had to think. Maybe she had become completely unglued by being on that program.

I heard dogs barking before I reached her house. It got worse when I knocked lightly on her door. If she didn't hear me, I could turn around and run home.

The door opened. Some of the dogs rushed out. Mrs. Landsdorf stood there smiling. "Hello, my dear friend," she said.

I walked in. A man was sitting in a chair. He got up, took three huge steps across the room, and shook my hand. He was wearing a cowboy hat, boots, and a suit with some fringe on it. He looked rich, but in a different way than Blake Reynolds IV.

"I'm Big Jed Buchanan," he said. "And you should be mighty proud of what you did for this little lady. Why, if you hadn't got her on

that TV program, I might never have learned about all of her Dobermans."

"Jed's setting me up in the breeding business," said Mrs. Landsdorf. "We're calling it *Dementia's Dobies*. Like it? And he's going to market my protein drink for dogs."

"I've been hankering for a venture like this for a long time," said Mr. Buchanan.

I kept looking at the man. What was his angle?

"Jed says I'll get rich," said Mrs. Landsdorf. "He keeps getting rich over and over again, so he must know how to do it. But I only want to do right by my dogs."

"That's what impressed me about Dementia," said Mr. Buchanan. "Her devotion to Dobermans."

"We're going out to dinner to celebrate," said Mrs. Landsdorf, "and we want you to come."

I begged off and ran to the library instead. When I got there, I checked up on Mr. Buchanan. He's the thirty-sixth richest man in America.

· 22 ·

This is where I am right now. I'm getting more telephone calls than ever. And more mail. Because of Mrs. Landsdorf and Big Jed Buchanan. It's like a new wave of people suddenly discovered that I won the sweepstakes.

I'm best friends with Roseanne again. And I'm going to call Newton and see if I can get him back. I know I'll be sorry when I do. He'll start pestering me all over again. But he was my friend *before,* and that's what counts with me. Melissa is still writing poems to me. But I'm big about it. I read them before I tear them up.

I'm going to buy a very expensive present for Roseanne. I'm buying it with *my* money. When Mom and Dad found out what I did for Mrs. Landsdorf, they said they were proud of me. They say I can be trusted. They say the sweepstakes money is all mine, and they'll come to *me* when they want money. They're hinting about a boat.

I'm busy entering sweepstakes again. I don't know whether I should tell my parents my latest news. Today in the mail I was officially informed that I won a prize in the MAKE-A-MINT SWEEPSTAKES. I am now the owner of a genuine aluminum key chain.

I think I can handle that.